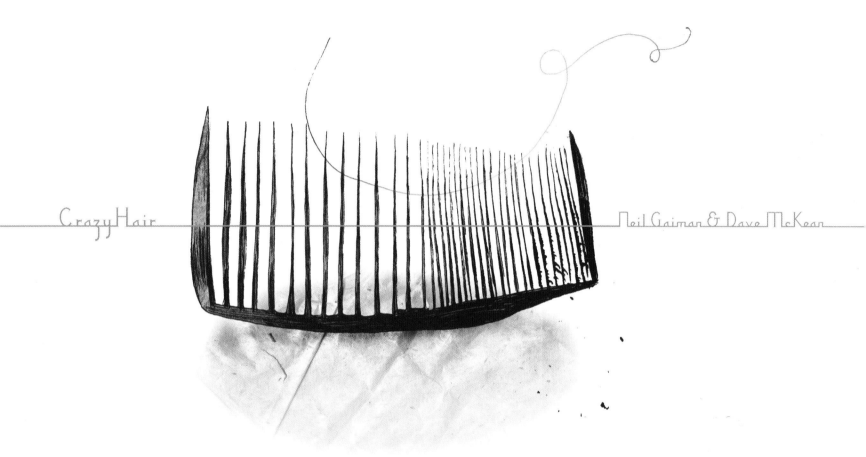

Crazy Hair

Neil Gaiman & Dave McKean

For Maddy

Bloomsbury Publishing, London, Berlin and New York
First published in Great Britain in August 2009 by Bloomsbury Publishing Plc
36 Soho Square, London, W1D 3QY
The paperback edition first published in 2010
First published in the USA in 2009 by HarperCollins Children's Books,
a division of HarperCollins Publishers, 1350 Avenue of the Americas, NY 10019
Published by arrangement with HarperCollins Children's Books,
a division of HarperCollins Publishers
Text copyright © by Neil Gaiman 2005, 2009
Illustrations copyright © by Dave McKean 2009
The moral rights of the author and illustrator have been asserted

A CIP catalogue record of this book is available from the British Library
Hardback ISBN 978 0 7475 9526 7
10 9 8 7 6 5 4 3
Paperback ISBN 978 0 7475 9599 1
10 9 8 7 6 5 4 3 2 1
Typography by Dave McKean
Printed in Italy by L.E.G.O. Spa, Vicenza
All papers used by Bloomsbury Publishing are natural, recyclable products made
from wood grown in well-managed forests. The manufacturing processes conform to
the environmental regulations of the country of origin
www.bloomsbury.com/childrens
www.gaimanmckeanbooks.co.uk

BLOOMSBURY

LONDON BERLIN NEW YORK

hair."

Crazy hair?
Oh me, oh my.
Crazy hair?
I thought I'd die.

Butterflies and
Cockatoos
Reds and yellows
Greens and blues

Make me look
Beyond compare

Walking with my crazy hair.

In my hair
Gorillas leap,
Tigers stalk,
And ground sloths sleep.
Prides of lions
Make their lair
Somewhere

in my *crazy hair.*

Hunters send in
Expeditions,
Radio back
Their positions

Still, we've lost
A dozen there
Lost inside my *crazy hair.*

They play tunes
Beyond compare,
Dancing through my crazy hair.

Huge balloons
Come down to land.   People wave.
It's very grand.

They take off
From everywhere,

Drift across my crazy hair.

There are pools
And water slides
Carousels
And pony rides

All the fun
Of any fair
Waits inside my crazy hair.

Twisting tangling
Trails and loops,
Treasure chests
And pirate sloops,

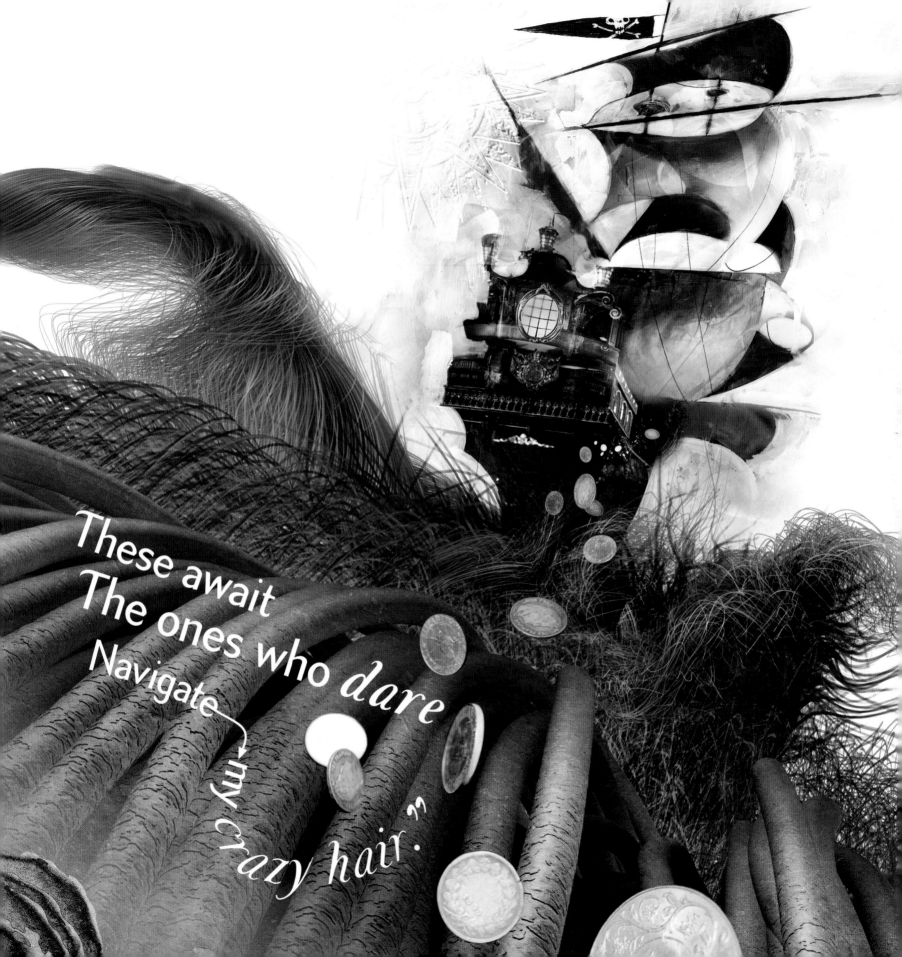

These await
The ones who dare
Navigate
my crazy hair."

That's what I do
With great care
When I have such *crazy hair*."

"Child! Are you mad!"

I cried.

"Combs and brushes

Have been tried.

One was eaten

By a bear

Prowling through my crazy hair."

crazy hair. "

I bent down
And Bonnie swiped
Combed and curried
Rubbed and wiped.

Came a
rumbling
from my hair.

One huge growling
Head peered out.
Said, "What is this
All about?"

One huge arm
Reached out of there —
Pulled her in my crazy hair.

Riding slides
And great balloons,
Finding hunters,
Losing moons,

Playing with
The pretty birds,
Teaching parrots
Naughty words,

Sewing up
The pirates' vests
Digging buried
Treasure chests,

Hibernating with the bear

Dancing with the dancers there

Happy as a millionaire,

Safe inside my *crazy hair*.